We're Very Good Friends,

My Sister and I

P. K. Hallinan

With special thanks to Margrit Fiddle

First printing this edition 2002

ISBN 0-8249-5386-X

Published by Ideals Children's Books
An imprint of Ideals Publications
A division of Guideposts
535 Metroplex Drive, Suite 250
Nashville, Tennessee 37211
www.idealsbooks.com

Printed and bound in Mexico by RR Donnelley.

Library of Congress CIP Data on file

10 9 8 7 6 5 4 3 2 1

ideals children's books™
Nashville, Tennessee

We're very good friends,
my sister and I.

We like to play games
and dress up like spies.

And sometimes we just don't
see eye to eye—
but that's okay,
we're friends anyway.

We do lots of fun things,
my sister and I.

We build fancy forts
with cardboard and tape.

We fly all around
in our magical capes.

We even make monsters
from old paper bags

and dress up like mummies
in bedsheets and rags.

We're pretty good mummies,
my sister and I.

And sometimes we'll stay
in the house for the day,
just singing and dancing
the hours away.

Or sometimes we'll spend
the whole day in the yard,
and make up new words
and laugh very hard.

We have wonderful times,
my sister and I.

We like to take hikes
through valleys and fields.

We like to ride bikes,
with cards on our wheels.

We even like helping
with chores when we can,
like sweeping up grease
from the old frying pan.

But then there are times when we need to discuss the things that are really important to us.

We work well together
when the work is too tough.

We stick close together
when the going gets rough.

And it goes without saying
that deep down we feel
our friendship is honest . . .
and lasting . . . and real.

So even at times
when we've had a big fight,
we don't ever worry—
we know it's all right.

'Cause nothing can alter
the love in our hearts

22

and nothing can drive us
or pry us apart.

We're joined at the soul,
and that's the best reason why

we're very good friends,
my sister and I.